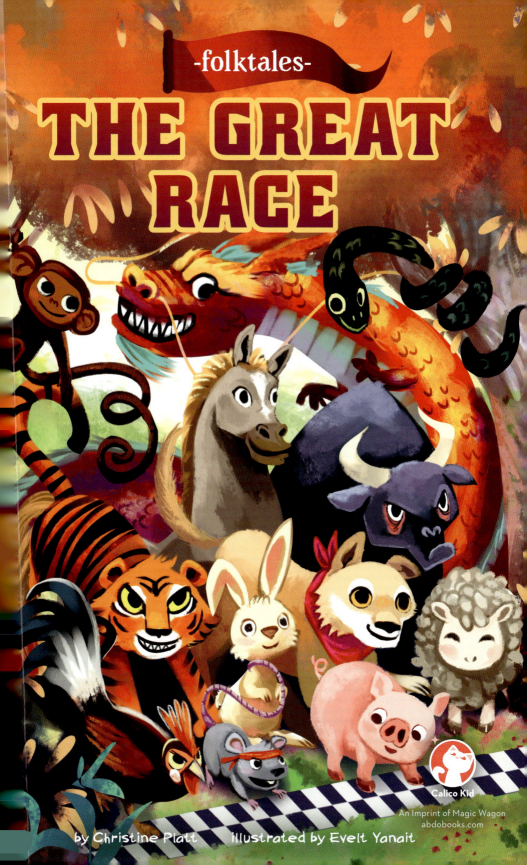

About the Author
Christine A. Platt is an author and scholar of African and African-American history. A beloved storyteller of the African diaspora, Christine enjoys writing historical fiction and non-fiction for people of all ages. You can learn more about her and her work at christineaplatt.com.

For the storytellers who capture and preserve histories--thank you! —CP

To Edgard and Alicia, for their endless love and care —EY

abdobooks.com

Published by Magic Wagon, a division of ABDO, PO Box 398166, Minneapolis, Minnesota 55439. Copyright © 2021 by Abdo Consulting Group, Inc. International copyrights reserved in all countries. No part of this book may be reproduced in any form without written permission from the publisher. Calico Kid™ is a trademark and logo of Magic Wagon.

Printed in the United States of America, North Mankato, Minnesota.
052021
092021

THIS BOOK CONTAINS RECYCLED MATERIALS

Written by Christine Platt
Illustrated by Evelt Yanait
Edited by Tyler Gieseke
Art Directed by Candice Keimig

Library of Congress Control Number: 2020948575

Publisher's Cataloging-in-Publication Data

Names: Platt, Christine, author. | Yanait, Evelt, illustrator.
Title: The great race / by Christine Platt : illustrated by Evelt Yanait
Description: Minneapolis, Minnesota : Magic Wagon, 2022 | Series: Folktales
Summary: Twelve animals race to determine where they will stand on the Chinese zodiac calendar, and each animal's unique quality comes into play!
Identifiers: ISBN 9781098230241 (lib. bdg.) | ISBN 9781098230807 (ebook) | ISBN 9781098231088 (Read-to-Me ebook)
Subjects: LCSH: Folk literature, Chinese--Juvenile literature. | Zodiac--Juvenile literature. | Animals--Juvenile literature. | Running races--Juvenile literature. | Folktales--Juvenile literature.
Classification: DDC 398.2--dc23

Table of Contents

Chapter #1
A Special Honor
4

Chapter #2
Ready, Set, Go!
12

Chapter #3
Middle of the Pack
20

Chapter #4
Last Leg
26

Chapter #1
A SPECIAL HONOR

Many years ago in China, Jade Emperor invited all the animals in the world to compete in a great race. He promised that the winner would receive a high honor.

Of all the animals, best friends Rat and Cat were most excited.

"Be sure to come and wake me up for the race tomorrow," Cat said. "I don't want to oversleep!" Sleeping was Cat's favorite activity.

"Of course," Rat said with a smile. "That's what friends are for."

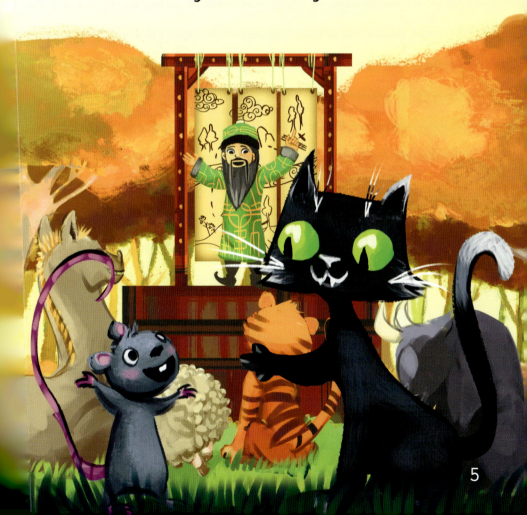

Other animals decided to join the race too. Snake would try to outwit his opponents. Speed would be Horse's strength. And Monkey was skilled at swinging in trees.

That evening, the animals all went to bed dreaming of the many prizes the winner might earn. They were so thrilled that they couldn't think of anything else.

Jade Emperor was eager to see how many animals would participate in his great race. To everyone's surprise, just twelve showed up the next morning. Some thought the race would be canceled. Instead, Jade Emperor had an idea.

"Every animal that showed up today will receive a high honor," he declared. "You will each win a spot on the Chinese zodiac calendar based on the order you cross the finish line. Every twelve years, people around the world will celebrate you."

The animals were delighted. Now the great race would be even more important.

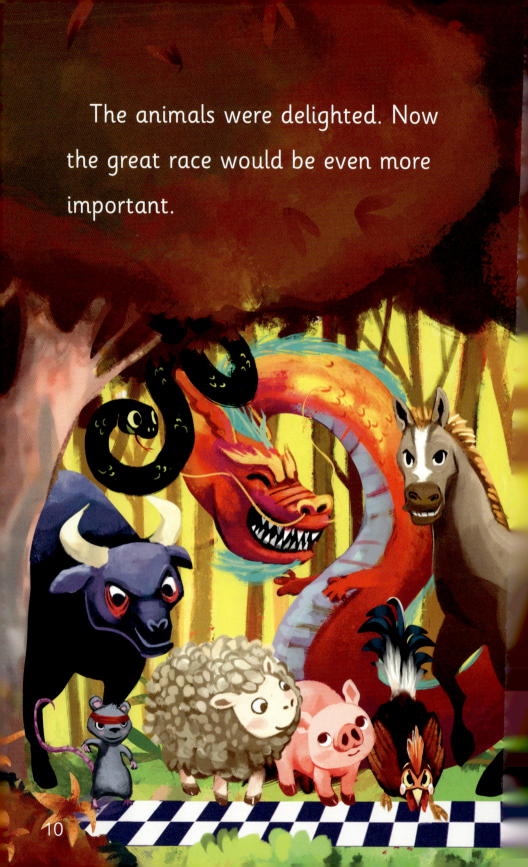

As Jade Emperor announced that the race was about to begin, each animal wondered which would come in first place. And each wondered which would be last.

They all lined up at the starting line.

Chapter #2
READY, SET, GO!

"Ready, set?" Jade Emperor asked.

He waited. "Go!"

And all of the animals went.

The race was very difficult. The animals had to run through a forest. They jumped over rocks and climbed the tallest trees. At the end was the biggest challenge of all—a vast river.

No animal received special treatment. No matter an animal's size or whether the animal could swim, each had to cross. The finish line was on the other side.

Rat and Ox reached the river first. Because Rat was small, he was exhausted. But he was also very cunning.

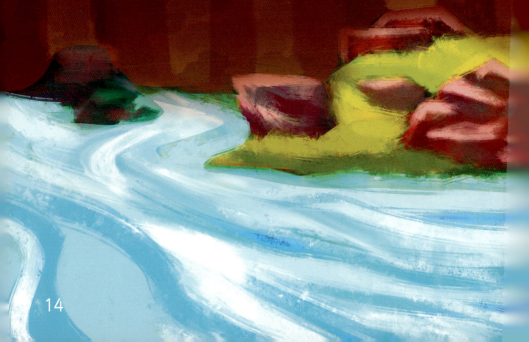

"Ox, could I sit on your head as you swim?" Rat asked politely. "I am so small that I'll never make it without help!"

Ox saw no harm in helping little Rat, so he said, "Of course!"

But as soon as they reached the other side, Rat hopped off Ox's head and sprinted over the finish line. So, Ox comes after Rat on the Chinese zodiac calendar.

Tiger was close behind, and he was a good swimmer. But he wasn't as fast as Ox. So, he came in third place.

Rabbit tried his best to swim as fast as he could. But he tired quickly. When he was about to give up, he climbed onto a log and drifted to shore. Rabbit was exhausted but also excited he wasn't last.

Eight more animals to go!

Chapter #3
MIDDLE OF THE PACK

Dragon was close behind Rabbit. He had even started out in the lead. But dragons are very helpful creatures. When he saw a village on fire, Dragon left the race to save the villagers. He used his strong breath to blow out the flames.

When he returned to the race, Rabbit was just ahead of him. Rabbit didn't know it, but Dragon once again used his breath—this time, to help send Rabbit's log to shore. Dragon was pleased to take fifth place.

Horse thought he could win. He was a strong runner and swimmer. But when he got to the river, he realized five others had already finished!

Desperately, he leapt into the water. Horse was so focused on the race that he didn't notice when Snake wrapped himself around one of Horse's legs.

Snake was crafty. When Horse reached the shoreline, Snake yelled, "Hiss!"

"Oh my!" Horse was so frightened that he forgot about the race for a minute. Snake left him in shock and slithered across the finish line. Horse soon galloped into seventh place.

The animals waited eagerly to see which racer would finish next.

Chapter #4
LAST LEG

Sheep, Monkey, and Rooster reached the river a little ahead of Pig and Dog. Sheep knew the three in the lead were not strong swimmers. "Why don't we work together?" he said to Monkey and Rooster. "Then we can be certain none of us comes in last." Monkey and Rooster liked Sheep's idea.

Quickly, they gathered as many branches as they could and made a raft. Happily, they drifted toward the other side.

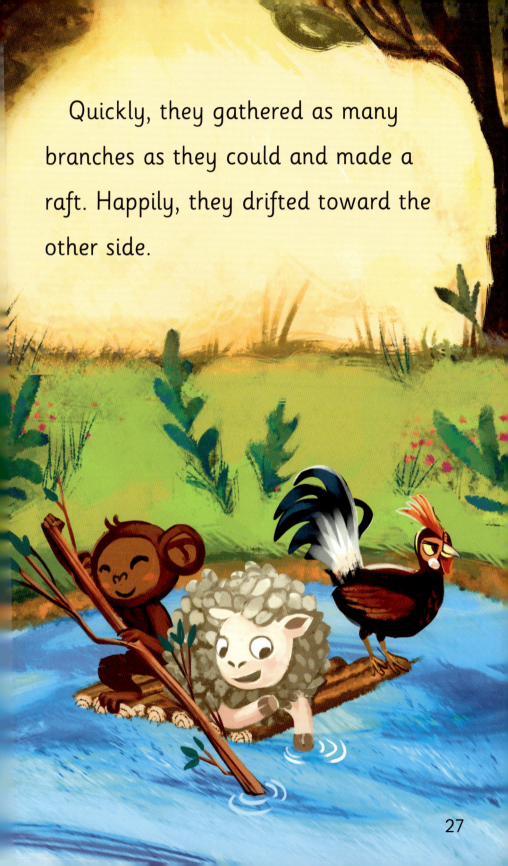

Near the shore, the three animals smiled at one another. "Time to make a run for it! May the fastest animal win."

Sheep arrived in eighth place. Monkey swung across the finish line next.

"Cock-a-doodle-doo!" Rooster cried out as he came in tenth.

Jade Emperor and the others looked to see whether Dog or Pig would be next. But they only saw Dog in the river.

"Where is Pig?" they all asked when Dog took eleventh place.

"We were swimming side by side," Dog explained. "But Pig smelled a delicious meal and went to get a bite. The last time I saw Pig, he was napping in the sunshine."

Rat thought of someone else who liked to nap. *Uh oh!* he thought. *I was so excited about the great race, I forgot to do something very important.*

When Pig finally crossed the finish line to take the last place on the Chinese zodiac calendar, the animals cheered loudly.

The noise woke Cat, who was sleeping in the village.

"That Rat!" Cat meowed angrily. "He didn't wake me up because he knew I'd come in first place. Wait until I see him!"

To this day, Rat and Cat are no longer best friends. Cat makes certain that he chases after Rat every chance he gets!